Letters
to
Phoenix

Letters to Phoenix

***

Julie Deshtor

ARCHWAY
PUBLISHING

Archway Publishing books may be ordered through booksellers or by contacting:

Archway Publishing
1663 Liberty Drive
Bloomington, IN 47403
www.archwaypublishing.com
1-(888)-242-5904

ISBN: 978-1-4808-1254-3 (sc)
ISBN: 978-1-4808-1255-0 (e)

Library of Congress Control Number: 2014919059

Printed in the United States of America.

Archway Publishing rev. date: 11/12/2014

Dedicated to all those who have ever lived in captivity, been torn away from those they love, or suffered an irrevocable loss of self.

Contents

Acknowledgments

I would like to thank my family for all these years of putting up with me, for encouraging my writing pursuits, and being there for me through everything. The same goes out to all my friends, who have throughout the years offered their support and their time. Special thanks to Jon, Raymond, Rachel, Jared, Chris, Wally, Kathy, Azrael, Rypa, Lee, Steve, Josh, Robert, Vadim, Dana, Miriam and Eli, and anyone else I may have failed to mention by name. I couldn't have done this without you.

Special Status Staff Buddy Suicide Risk Run Risk

To shed your skin. To crack your skull against a wall you cannot walk through no matter how many times you split your skull open against it.

To be alone. To be tucked away so well, hidden so safely, that even you yourself do not know where you are.

To watch the years crawl by until freedom is no longer a gift, just a fact full of memories.

To watch from a distance.

He was Phoenix.

Chapter 1

He had nowhere to go besides that place, having been committed to the program. He was sixteen.

Six days after he arrived there, his birthday came. Emma didn't come. All the boys were out on the field playing football. He thought he saw her car on the road that day, a white two-door apparition that he chased in a frenzy. The orderlies chased after him. He caught up with the car only to see a stranger's face behind the wheel. One of the men caught up with him. He snapped and took all his fear and frustration out on the orderly. The rest he didn't remember, though he could imagine the crackle of bones shattering. He spent his birthday in an adult jail cell.

After three days he was released back to the Farmstead, into seclusion. The seclusion room had been converted from a basement bedroom. The sturdy old-fashioned windowsill was once intended as a shelf, so that plants, or pictures, could be placed along the window. Since then, the glass had been replaced with the thick bulletproof kind, and the windowsill now supported an oak board of equal thickness. Someone had been thoughtful enough to drill holes the size of a quarter through the wood to allow thick long beams of sunlight inside.

The sun only hurt his eyes.

He didn't remember to eat or sleep. All he could see, like a playback video loop, was her car – tiny, white, lost on the dirt road. It didn't matter that it turned out to be someone else's car. It didn't matter that it wasn't Emma behind the steering wheel.

He practiced his punches on the oak board, driving the splinters deep in-between the knuckles. Twelve days into his seclusion the Farmstead owner, George, was forced to replace the steel door into the room. It was dented and warped, shaky from the boy's full-body assaults. *If only I could break through*, he thought, *nothing in the world would keep me here.* The door became his adversary. He battered it like a ram, slamming his forehead over and over against the tempered metal. Eventually, the steel started caving in, losing its elasticity. He'd cracked his skull open a few times, but that didn't seem to register in a brain overridden with panic and claustrophobia.

Out of twenty-three days spent in seclusion, the boy visited the emergency room a total of seven times.

Chapter 2

Emma sat on the brown checkered couch in the high school student counseling office, and stared out of the window at the crystalline snow that descended onto the ground below. The school counselor, Janna, had stepped out, and so Emma waited for a long time, almost the entire lunch hour, before the office door finally opened. Janna was a slight, thin woman, with wild red hair, freckles and a Ph.D. in psychology. She took one look at Emma's face, furrowed her eyebrows, and said, "Come on in. Let's talk."

"He's gone," Emma sobbed out in the private back room and hurriedly laid out the whole story. Early Saturday morning she had pulled up to his house only to have his parents tell her that he wasn't there. She didn't believe what she had heard. He may have been late before, but he had never stood her up. The last time her mom was in Rio, Emma had expected him around six. It wasn't until eight thirty that he finally rang her doorbell. His hair was wet and tangled, and his forehead glistened from the melting snow, but his eyes sparkled in triumph as he told her that he had walked to her house.

He lived half a city away.

***

There was no way he simply had blown off their plans for the day. Politely, she asked his mother if everything was okay. His mother began crying softly and shook her head no.

"What's going on, Lida?" Emma demanded. "Where is he?"

"Derek's not here." His stepdad came to the door. "Look here, Emma, we don't know where he's gone, or when he'll be back."

The only other clue she was able to gather consisted of the words "Boys' Farmstead." These were whispered to her by his best friend, Brandon, who managed to sneak a quick phone call from his mother's house where he sat, grounded for his association with the two of them. She repeated those words to Janna, hoping that the counselor might be able to make sense of whatever was going on.

Janna just shook her head. "I used to work at one of those places, long ago. Honestly, I didn't like their philosophy, or methods." She interrupted Emma's question. "They're teen behavior correctional facilities."

"But he hasn't done anything!"

"I know, sweetheart. They're private programs; his parents must've sent him there."

Emma stared at the woman, wide-eyed. "Sent him there? Doesn't there have to be a crime, a court order, something?"

Janna smiled a sad smile. "It's really up to the parents; they don't need any specific medical or legal cause," she shrugged her shoulders, "though I'm not convinced that that's the best solution when it comes to problem teens."

"How long will he be there?"

"Insurance will pay for a twenty-eight day evaluation. After that, parents pay out of their own pockets."

Janna was one of Emma's favorite teachers, competent and fair, and Emma trusted her experience. The girl took a deep breath. It was going to be okay. His parents didn't have much money.

***

Before Janna finally settled as a counselor and psychology teacher at the private high school, she had worked at several psychiatric wards and treatment centers. The captivating, no-nonsense teacher enlivened her lessons with vivid stories from her own field experience.

"Schizophrenia," Janna explained to her students, "is often confused with Multiple Personality Disorder, though they have nothing in common. MPD isn't even accepted by mainstream psychiatry, while a schizophrenia diagnosis is a very real tragedy. Schizophrenic patients cease to be themselves. With medication, a patient may get better in time and may even be able to function normally, but as an entirely different person. A family forever loses their loved one."

The story that stood out the most in Emma's mind was about a catatonic boy, a teenager about her own age that Janna had once worked with. The boy never moved in his bed; the staff fed him through a tube, changed him and turned him, while Janna, still an intern, was in charge of his exercise routine.

At noon every day, Janna wheeled the boy out to the yard and stood him up on the grass. He would stand motionlessly wherever he was placed, eyes inverted into himself. Janna would grab a football out of the basket and walk away, counting her steps out loud. At exactly twenty-five steps Janna would stop, face the patient, and throw him the ball.

His eyes would not move, not a single muscle would twitch, no flicker of interest would cross his face. Still, as the ball shot past his face, his right hand would suddenly spring up and stop the ball's trajectory. There he would remain, a lifeless statue of a boy with his right arm up above his head, his fingers triumphantly clutching the football.

That was the catatonic stage of the cycle, Janna explained. Next came the psychotic one.

The day the boy came back to life he sat up suddenly in his bed, alarming the nurses who had cared for him. Janna was alerted to his awakening by a bloodcurdling scream coming from the boy's room. The nurse that had rushed to assist the patient was rewarded with a savage bite to her left ear. She wailed. Blood poured down the side of her head, stained her baby blue scrubs and dripped onto the immaculate tile floor. The boy sat up in his bed, wide-eyed and dazed, with the nurse's shredded earlobe hanging from his lips.

The boy was sent home to his family as soon as he recovered from the psychotic episode. He remembered nothing of the incident. "The cycle had begun anew," Janna told her students.

Chapter 3

The town folk didn't have much liking for the Farmstead boys. There were tales around town of the boys vandalizing locals' houses, stealing their cars. There were also stories of the boys raping the local girls. Whenever a new boy arrived at the Farmstead, the farmers made a point of lining the main street and staring the stranger down as he rode through town. They talked amongst themselves, pointed their fingers, wrinkled their foreheads.

This boy's arrival was even more memorable. He came all the way up the canyon boxed in an old truck by two of the Farmstead orderlies, and surrounded by an "honorary escort."

***

At eight thirty that morning two men had knocked on his parents' door, acting as truancy officers. He was awake; he was expecting Emma to come pick him up around nine. She'd told him that her mother was going out of town for the entire day and night, so he spent his morning daydreaming about Emma's daybed with the cast iron bars, the delicate skin of her neck, her small hands.

When the two men showed up at the door, he wasn't alarmed. He had, after all, been recklessly skipping school. The sun shone prettily that morning, reflecting off the mushy snow in the driveway. His spirits were high, and he went along with the two officers that wanted to chat with him about his attendance. He figured he was going to be back just in time. Emma was always a few minutes late.

***

Halfway up to the Farmstead, long after he realized what was happening, he bolted. He used an old trick on the two guards. "I have to pee. I have to pee. I have to pee right now!"

They stopped the truck, let him out. He did his thing, zipped up his fly, and then he was gone.

He headed straight for the freeway, cutting through the midday traffic, the smoke from the rubber of the wheels, the cussing. He ran north at first, then west, back home. In his head, he counted how many times his feet touched the ground. *One, two, three, eighteen, twenty-nine, ninety-eight, two thousand.* A sharp pain in the left side of his gut was making it hard to concentrate, and at four thousand and thirty-three, he lost count. His eyes were blurry from the sweat that rolled down his forehead. He no longer knew which way he was running, but he did not dare stop. After a while, he wound up on the freeway again and ran alongside it, with all his might, downhill. He could hear his footsteps bouncing off the concrete, could feel the ground flying back underneath him. When he came around the bend of the road, it took him a second to register what he saw. And when it finally did register, the boy had no option but to stop and wait for the highway patrolman to catch up with him.

***

The new boy rode through the town with a sheriff's car in front of the truck, and the highway patrol right behind it. The town folk really had something to talk about that evening.

Chapter 4

"Twenty-eight days," Janna had told her. Emma started a journal that very day. The first entry read:

"Phoenix,

I pray to the Christian God, he who has forsaken us, to spare you, and to shield you from the awful truth of the world. May the skies always be starry for you, and may the wind be wild, and may the sun always shine for you in the afternoons. In pain and in hope, I pray to the God of Righteousness to shield you from the light, and to keep your spirit intact. May your hair always be dark and plentiful, and may your hands never wither. I pray, also, to the forces of darkness and fire, which have fathered you, to protect you, and to deliver you forth from the terrible goodness of God. I bid the owls and mosquitoes to carry my love to you, so you may return unharmed to our sweet neverland."

***

Twenty-two days later, Emma's mother received a phone call from the state police. The officer demanded to speak with Emma.

"My daughter had nothing to do with this," Natalia said firmly. "You won't harass my child in this manner." She hung up the phone.

"Derek is missing." She looked at Emma blankly. "First they lock their own kid up. Then they misplace him and have the nerve to blame mine!" Suddenly, Natalia's eyes regained focus. She glared at her daughter.

"You didn't have anything to do with this, did you?"

Emma silently shook her head, avoiding her mother's eyes. She had had nothing to do with this, though she wished she had. Not that it mattered, now that he had finally broken free.

"They can't hold you, Phoenix, there's no cage fit for you in this world," Emma whispered into the cool night air, as she lay in her bed that night. She pictured his face. She pictured his lips. She pictured the blue fire of his eyes. She listened for footsteps outside her window.

Chapter 5

No one could quite figure out how he'd managed to bypass the alarms and the thick steel bars on the windows and doors. There was nowhere for him to go; just the woods and the fields that stretched around for miles. No cars in town, or Farmstead horses, for that matter, were missing. Yet the boy was gone.

George called the police and notified his family. He even had the cops call his girlfriend's house, threatening her with criminal prosecution, accusing her mother of harboring a runaway.

For three days and nights the small town remained on red alert. Folks locked their doors at night. Canine units combed the woods, and highway patrol patrolled the roads. A rescue helicopter was brought in, disturbing the town folk at night with its spotlight. Still, there was no trace of the missing boy.

The search may have gone on indefinitely, if, on the third day, he hadn't gotten hungry and cold.

He sat up in the gutter alongside the football field directly in front of the facility.

Chapter 6

Emma's days were spent driving wide circles around his parents' house. The motion itself was exhilarating, giving her a sense of purpose. The streets gave her hope. At every turn of the road, she expected to see him walking home. Everything around her was permeated with his presence; she couldn't shake him off. Even her route home from school went right past the high school he had gone to for a total of seven months.

He had told Emma that he hated his school, hated being separated from her, hated the way she kept him from lashing out against the pink, well-dressed sophomores who found amusement in his strangeness. He'd spend his nights reading *The Catcher in the Rye* or *The Master and Margarita*, then compensate by sleeping in class. Emma urged him to stay in school, to stay out of trouble. She believed in his academic abilities; he was smart enough to get good grades. She was the valium to his rage.

The moment the final bell rang, he'd bolt outside and scan the parking lot for her little white car. On the days her own school schedule permitted it, Emma was there, car door flung wide open, "…you destroyed the world, but we are still here, we will nurse our hurt, we'll grow strong on tears ..." blaring from the stock speakers. On the days she couldn't make it, he walked home.

***

Once, he had told Emma that he wished he could attend a private school like her, where the kids could read and teachers gave a damn. On a few occasions, he even joined her in her ceramics class, with her instructor's permission. He used to inhabit the wall nearest to her work table and remain there, a silent gargoyle, for the entire two hours of the class. His muscles froze, his eyes grew vacant, almost entirely unblinking. People would bump into him, try to talk to him, shove him. He wouldn't move. Only the sound of her voice would awaken him from the catatonic trance.

***

Even now, in class, she still half-expected to turn around and see him there, waiting.

He wasn't there.

And so she'd skip school to zigzag through his old neighborhood. Her eyes, red and swollen from endless crying, conjured up apparitions of him in the streets. She chased those for hours, never catching up and never losing sight of the ghost, until at eight at night her curfew demanded her home.

Chapter 7

The boy stood by the barrack window. The steel bars in the frame were a fire hazard, but no one seemed to care. The bars were merely a confirmation. *My wings mean nothing. I am trapped.*

He waited, peering into the dark. His fingers crushed a cigarette filter. He searched for a white shape on the old farmstead road, listened for the rustle of tires against the gravel. His legs were cramping. He felt as if he was growing into the land, sprouting roots. He could sense the ghosts within the landscape, ancient spirits. He prayed to them. *Find her, guide her.*

A spider was crawling along one of the metal rods, and the boy could almost guess its thoughts. It didn't seem to care about the spirits shifting beneath the newly deposited soil. What bothered it instead was the thick, foul smoke clogging its sensitive smellers. It could barely breathe, encased in the sticky cloud, and its hardy chitin armor was beginning to itch. Looking positively alarmed, the creature resorted to excreting tiny clear droplets that glimmered in the moonlight and thickened to stretchy goo immediately upon hitting the night air. Thus, the small arachnid retreated in indignant haste.

The boy watched the miniature commotion with a smile. He swallowed the last drag of his cigarette and flicked the butt through a crack in the glass. His movement was precise; the filter flew through the crack and landed in the grass beyond the bars. He watched the spider freeze on its tiny thread and pictured a furry head vanishing between eight huddled shoulders. He laughed softly and to himself. No one heard him, none of the other boys, or the head orderly, Mark, asleep in his room at the end of the hallway. Only the spider heard. It hurried along.

The boy knew so much. He knew that in the morning one of the kids assigned to outside chores would conveniently remove the incriminating, tar-soaked cylinder. He knew that Mark had again forgotten to arm the alarm system. He knew, by name, the spirits beneath the desecrated land. He knew each constellation in the sky. He knew of impotence and fear.

What he didn't know was how to reach Emma.

Chapter 8

Finally, Emma got up the courage to call his parents. She wanted to send him a late birthday present, so he would know that she was out there, waiting.

His mother had to think about it first.

"Sure. I am sure that would be fine."

Emma wanted to send him three separate things: something special, something practical, and a card. The mall, though vibrant with human bustle and "sale" signs, had nothing to offer. She looked up an eclectic gift shop in the phone book. There, under the compassionate eye of an old lady in a purple scarf, Emma found her treasures. She bought him a pendant, that of a phoenix, silver and delicately crafted, to remind him of what he was. She ached to lend him strength, somehow. She found the perfect card: a green field with tiny blue and yellow flowers, a lone wolf in the field, her gaze lost in the skies, and above her, an enormous eagle, his wings spread across the horizon, his shadow caressing the wolf with a few stray feathers. "I love you. I am here. It's okay," Emma wrote. For the practical item, she picked clove gum. She figured that he couldn't smoke his clove cigarettes, wherever he was. She hoped the gum would ease the cravings and remind him of home.

Emma hummed to herself as she wrapped the precious gifts. Tears rolled down her face and dripped off the tip of her nose. She flew to his parents' home; eager, flustered and so hopeful she knocked on their door. They opened the door for her and accepted the small package. She thanked them over and over, holding her hands to her chest. As she drove away, she pictured him opening the package, clutching the silver pendant in his hand, tenderly, as if she were there with him.

Chapter 9

He treasured each of the few things that he had left of Emma.

There was the shirt she'd made for him just a few days before he was sent away. She took a black T-shirt and drew an outline of a phoenix with orange nail polish on the back, and the infinity symbol on the front. He was wearing it when he was first picked up and had managed to hide it before it was confiscated. He also had his school bag with him that day and in it a notepad that the orderlies didn't look through all the way before deeming it harmless. On the back few pages, in small feathery letters, she'd scribbled her poems.

When he was first assigned a bunk in one of the boys' bedrooms, he hid the torn-out pages between the bed frame and the box spring. He only took them out at night, after making sure that his roommate was asleep. He couldn't make out the letters in the dark, but that didn't matter. He knew every line, every turn of her pencil. He memorized each word. Late at night, through the wasteland silence and the rustle of the snow, he could almost hear her voice:

I am god.

I created you.

You are a dream.

My dream.

My life.

My loneliness.

Personified.

Chapter 10

There was an aching void in Emma's world, a painful absence, as if she were an amputee. The phantom limb throbbed, giving her no peace. With him gone, she was left crippled. She went about her life blindly, stumbling at every turn, straining to hear. His ghost hung about her. In the little time they had spent together, their lives became entangled. Each wore the other's scent like a brand.

Emma used memories like bandages. The memories became her crutch; the images of his bed in a cluttered room with two entrances and no doors that once had replaced the world for the two of them. The black and white murals he'd painted on his bedroom walls, images of fantastic beings, of angels and gargoyles, of things with sharp teeth and claws and wings.

In the cold winter afternoons he used to shut out the outside light with heavy black drapes. The black and white murals on his walls would come to life, howling, baring their fangs, tender sensitive ears twitching at the slightest noise: the sound of a child crying next door, the crispy crackle of careful footsteps outside his window, the squeaking of his parents' key in the front door lock. Those hours strained with magic. He was a statue carved of marble and she still remembered marveling at his beauty as she traced the line of his shoulders, around his throat, back towards the sharp points of his shoulder blades. His wings eclipsed the sky. It shone forth in his eyes only, a brilliant scrap of blue. His eyes held all the world's tenderness and loathing. He knew the answers to all her questions. She saw in him the demon of the waterless desert; he who had taught women to paint their faces.

***

She needed him; she craved his love and his darkness. She hoped his magic was enough. She didn't understand why he hadn't come for her, yet.

Chapter 11

About a month into his stay the boy finally met with the Farmstead therapist for an evaluation. Together, they went over the "issues" listed in his file, briefly touching on each item.

"Deviant behavior."

"Well," the therapist stated. "That's fairly self-explanatory." The boy grinned inwardly. On the outside, he seemed indifferent.

"Homosexual tendencies."

The therapist looked up and stared at the boy, but said nothing.

"Drug use."

The therapist looked back up, then cocked his head.

"Are you using drugs?" he asked.

"No." The boy scowled. "I smoke."

The therapist shook his head. "We'll see about that."

Thus, they came to the last item on the list.

"S & M tendencies," the paper read.

"S & M tendencies?" The therapist frowned. "What the hell is that supposed to mean? I've never heard of such a diagnosis." He looked the boy up and down, then looked into his eyes. "Hell, so you like it rough in the sack." He shrugged. "That's not a psychiatric condition. That's bullshit." The therapist struck the last item from the file with a thick purple marker.

The therapist's name was Dave.

Chapter 12

In her mind, Emma kept replaying the first night he'd spent at her house. It was snowing outside and he was late getting there.

Her mom flew back to Rio to spend the weekend with Emma's dad, so Emma invited all her friends over to party. They drank beer and watched movies all evening long.

Just after midnight, Emma pulled him aside. "Derek, don't you need to call your parents and check in?"

He looked at her, perplexed, shrugged his shoulders and picked up the phone.

"Mom? It's me. I won't be home tonight. No, I'm staying at a friend's house. You don't know her. No, it doesn't matter! Why? It's none of your fucking business!" He slammed the receiver down and grinned. Emma stood there in shock. She was hopelessly falling in love.

She locked everyone else out of her bedroom that night; and everyone grudgingly fell asleep. The two of them sat on her bed for hours. He played with her hair and the soft lace ribbons of her top, leafed through the old picture albums she pulled off the oak shelves. As the night crested, his shadow grew larger. His hair came undone; it curled around his face, sensual and so very black. The tips were dyed bright orange; the shade of hungry fire. She asked him why he'd dyed it that way. "It stands for what I am; Phoenix, creature of fire and ash." He smiled and whipped his hair around his face impatiently.

It took them three hours to undress, and when he finally pulled off her panties Emma straddled him with a swift movement because she was afraid that he would never pull her near. For a second, his magic came undone; his pupils dilated helplessly, his thin body contracted. But then he smiled and stretched under her and everything was okay again.

His skin was milk and vodka, his shoulders so white, that she could almost feel the marble when she touched him. Emma expected a boy's touch; he was almost a year younger than her. She was surprised when his arms locked behind her back, his fingertips kissed her shoulder blades, the nape of her neck, and he lifted her effortlessly and placed her on the bed. His hands shaped her body with perfect ease. All she managed to say was, "I didn't expect you to be this good."

He smiled darkly. "I've had the time to think of what I wanted to do to you."

His skin gleamed in the candlelight; the blue eyes shone with madness now. He didn't say anything else, so she didn't speak again, lost in his arms.

He didn't take her that night, and when she attempted to force him, he rolled down to the floor playfully, folded himself neatly under her bed and stared from under there with sky-blue innocent eyes.

"My monster under the bed," Emma laughed gently. She always felt a little safer sleeping after that night. In her dreams, a pair of blue-green, shiny eyes watched over her every move.

Chapter 13

It took three months for the Farmstead barber to finally cut the new boy's hair; three months and two orderlies holding him still.

The boy watched the long black strands fall, littering the floor around him.

He had fought so hard all this time, spent so many days staring at the world through the round holes of the seclusion room, that he almost felt a sense of relief now, when it was all over.

But Emma, she loved my hair.

She could brush it forever, running her fingers through the black silk. She believed that a man's life force, his sexuality, was in his hair; that cutting it equaled castration. "Remember the story of Samson and Delilah?" she asked him once. "It's no wonder men must keep their hair short in our sexless culture. Civility is built on impotence."

The boy watched the long black strands as they fell, and wondered – *was she right?*

Chapter 14

Twenty-eight days came and went, and still there was no word from him. His parents would tell her nothing. He hadn't contacted her yet, and Emma knew, always knew, that he would come for her if only he had the chance. She kept calling his parents, though she suspected they did not want to hear from her. But they held the answers; they were the thin thread connecting her to him now.

***

The twenty-eighth and final entry in her journal read:

"So many times I imagine you coming back, me running up to you, calling your name, you turning around, eyes afire, and catching me in your arms, holding me close... But what will happen, love? Will you turn away from me, perhaps, flashing the whiteness of your shoulders for the last time? Will you walk away? The scary part is that I love the madness in you, so much a part of you, like the smell of your clove cigarettes. Phoenix, Phoenix, Phoenix, the proud flame-bird, will they make you human again? Such a murderous crime, this..."

Chapter 15

All the boys at the Farmstead had roommates, two or four boys to a room. The Farmstead staff tried to bunk low-level kids with high-levels. The more experienced kids kept an eye on the troublemakers; this helped cut down on the costs. He was paired up with a kid about his own age, Ryan.

Ryan was a lifer at the Farmstead; he had been there since he was seven. His mother was an actress or a model or a whore; no one could ever quite tell from Ryan's elaborate stories. Whatever her career entailed, it left no time for a child.

The first thing Ryan noticed was his long nails. "Wow." He eyed them cautiously. "Are those real?" He inspected the claws with profound interest. "Have you ever tried sharpening them into a point?"

The boy hadn't, but since he had nothing better to do with his time, he sharpened them that very night.

***

The following morning, at breakfast, he was met with a low murmur from the line of kids awaiting their portions. He shrugged inwardly, picked up his tray and got in line. *You are all cardboard to me, anyway,* he thought, feeling nauseous. He wasn't hungry. Like an afterthought, a painful whisper came. *Where is she?* Then someone shoved him from behind.

The boy almost fell, but regained his balance, and bared his teeth. "Nice claws, Batman!" An oily, smooth face loomed over him. *Like a swine's snout,* he thought, detached. A tall kid, his head shaved clean and his trousers neatly creased, joined Pig-Face. "What's your name, sweetheart?" The kid's dry hand reached up to stroke his hair. The middle and index fingers had AB tattooed on them. "You're pretty." The tall kid drawled when he talked.

The boy held his ground, held his tray up like a shield, his back against the counter. He held back the hate that rose with the bile in his throat; the seductive urge to slam the edge of the tray into the grinning mouths, the yellow teeth before him, to shatter the plastic and use the shards to gouge out the staring eyes.

It'd been two days since he'd last gotten out of seclusion. He had been able to walk the yard, stretch his feet, feel the grass tickle his toes through the holes in his socks. Last night, he had slept on a mattress, warm under a blanket. He slept not far from the wrinkled pieces of paper that trapped a fraction of her soul. He breathed in her scent. It was a luxury he'd forgotten, and wasn't ready to give up again. And so he held still. He held his tray like a shield. He held his rage. He held back the sea of mindless, faceless grins.

"Derek!" Mark announced from the door. The sea broke up, formed into a semblance of a line. The orderly scanned the room, sensing a commotion. In his corner, the boy slowly lowered his tray. His hands were shaking. "Derek!" Finally, Mark's words registered. "You are wanted in the main office."

***

His first homecall.

The boy stared at the white apparatus before him and fought to gather his thoughts. What could he say to these people who pretended to love him, smiled to his face and schemed behind his back? Why would he want to talk to them, anyway? They have locked him up and conveniently forgotten about him.

And where was Emma?

The phone rang. The loud sound startled him. His hand was still shaking as he reached for the receiver.

"Derek? It's so good to hear your voice! We miss you so much, sweetheart." His mother's voice poured in like honey, bandaging his fear, familiar and warm. His stepdad joined in. "How are you doing, buddy?"

"Mom? How the hell do you think I'm doing? You need to come and get me, now!"

"Derek, we can't do that, buddy. I'm real sorry, but we can't." Gary went on in a gray monotone. "We're hearing you're doing better. They told us that we may be allowed to come visit you soon, if you keep up the good work."

"Gary, are you fucking deaf? Mom? Get me the fuck out of here!"

"Derek, honey, you don't need to get so upset. Your dad and I, we pray for you every day. You're always in our thoughts."

"Mom! Dad! Please? You don't understand! This place is hell!"

A click echoed somewhere along the wire. "I'm dying in here!" the boy shouted into the deaf receiver; into the long beeps on the other end.

The door opened. Dave walked in, frowning. "Something's wrong with the connection." He rested his hand on the boy's shoulder and flashed him a reassuring smile. "We'll try them back in a few days, okay?"

***

Still dazed, the boy wandered into his room. Most of the kids were out on chores. Sunlight streamed in through the window bars. He wrapped his arms around himself, stifling a sob. He stared out at the dirt road winding through the Farmstead gate. *Where are you?*

The boy glanced behind him, then quickly lifted up the box spring and pulled out a stack of papers – her poems, his unsent letters. He smoothed out a wrinkled page and whispered, "We are the monsters, we are the outcasts."

There was a rustling by the door. The boy spun around, shoving the papers under the mattress as he turned. Ryan was standing in the doorway.

"Did I startle you, bro?" Ryan walked up and placed both hands on the other boy's shoulders. "Don't trip about them, man." He nodded in the general direction of the kitchen. "Don't trip, okay? I've got your back."

Chapter 16

Emma threw open the door to Janna's office and fell on the checkered couch.

"It's been two months!"

"I don't understand." Janna flung her arms open, crossed the room and stopped right in front of the girl. "Could his parents have paid to keep him there?"

"With what? Food stamps?"

A silence hung in the room.

"Janna, where is he? What have they done to him?"

The woman slowly shook her head.

"I don't know, hon'. I'll see what I can find out."

Janna took a quick step forward, grabbed the girl by the hand and flipped her arm over. Her eyes narrowed.

"What is this, Emma? Have you lost your mind?"

The girl pulled her sleeve back down, covering the thin jagged line that wove its way up her arm, from her wrist to her elbow. "It's not what you think, Janna." Emma hid her face. "It's the not knowing. It hurts. I have to let it out somehow."

Janna sat down next to the girl and wrapped her in her shawl.

"I know, sweetheart, I know."

The counselor rocked the girl back and forth, humming a gentle tune, as one would to an infant. Her eyes were open wide, unblinking. She was looking out the window, past the glass and the overgrown aspens outside, past the fence encircling the school yard. Her eyelashes were glistening.

Chapter 17

The boy never ceased to surprise the Farmstead staff.

One night he took a disposable razor apart and used the blades to slice his wrists, just like he used to, for her, with her. The pain from the exposed meat of his arms brought him back to life. He could feel her tongue, soft and moist, flickering back and forth across the cuts. They even stung a little from her saliva. Her hand was so skilled and soft, exquisite within his memory. He imagined wrapping his own calloused hand around hers, matching rhythms. He closed his eyes and clung to the memories of sensation until, some thirty minutes later, he finally climaxed.

***

The following morning they took away all his clothes and assigned him a bright orange jumpsuit that read in front and on the back: "I am a runaway. Please call The Boys' Farmstead."

A staff member followed the boy everywhere he went, even when he had to use the toilet. His level dropped to SSSBSRRR – Special Status: Staff Buddy, Suicide Risk, Run Risk.

He laughed and laughed and laughed in the face of Jordan, a large, awkward man assigned to watch over him.

"Hey, Jordan, are you getting off watching me piss?" The laughter was bubbling out of him, spilling through the fingers of the hand with which he covered his mouth. "Run risk? Suicide risk?" He giggled, stuttered and grabbed at his ribs with his other hand, letting his pants fall to the floor.

"I was jacking off, jack-ass!"

Chapter 18

At night, alone in her room, Emma drowned in memories. She ached for him; she summoned him with all her strength. He used to give her purpose. He made her feel alive. He looked at her with such trust, such devotion, that she denied him nothing. He told her things that could be believed only in a dream. She told him everything, confessing her immediate need for physical pain, her alienation from the crowds all around her. He knew about her mother's endless curiosity, her writing, and all the loneliness she had collected over the years spent as a stranger in her own life. He received it all; her hectic tales of Rio de Janeiro, the dogs barking late at night at the abandoned warehouses, the motorcycle snarl as the gangs rushed past her bedroom windows. He listened to her music. How did it sound to him, the strange words loosely joined in a melody that held no meaning? He learned the lyrics – he would sing along.

And she, she was drunk on his madness. She would listen to his tales of contempt and rejection, marveling at his disregard for all social norms. He was unlike any of the boys who sought her interest. He didn't try to fit in, he didn't brag, he didn't lie. He had no place in the ordinary world.

"You are too beautiful." Emma would look into his eyes, searching for the truth. "You can't be real."

"I am real."

He was – his long black hair, his marble shoulders, his mad blue-green eyes.

For a while, the tribulations of the world left them alone, just like his parents did. On late afternoons, his mom and stepdad would take off to a movie and leave them both to themselves. "Will you two get the hell out of here, already?" He'd glare at Lida and Gary until they scrambled to find their coats, hiding their faces from his irate stare. Their smiles were shaky.

"You be good now, kids," they would say right before he'd slam the door in their faces.

Emma used to lie awake in bed at night and listen to the rain drumming against the skylights. She used to wonder if he was somewhere out there, in the streets. He was her miracle, her creation. She'd summoned him from another world, where he was Phoenix, and she was never alone.

***

She was alone now, and the streets were barren.

Chapter 19

It must've been three in the morning when the boys were woken by George shining a flashlight in their eyes. He was accompanied by Jordan.

"Out in the hall, now!" George barked. The boys sat up on their bunks, winced at the bright light, and slowly, sleepily obeyed. They stood in the hallway, exchanging uncertain glances, shivering, shifting from one bare foot to the other. The low-level kids were not allowed to have shoes, unless they were doing outside chores or working at the Farmstead. "I'd rather put up with the trouble of having the boys working on my farmstead than deal with illegals," George used to joke. "Physical labor is good for the boys, it disciplines them, teaches them responsibility and the value of a hard day's work." The high-level kids, on the other hand, had access to their shoes; they could come and go at will during the day, though at night their shoes, too, were locked up with the rest. It seemed to the boy that every kid at the Farmstead scrambled to gain and keep his levels. The only way to achieve that was to do as you were told and make sure those around you did the same. The boy refused to be a part of that game; he was above the sniveling and snitching.

***

When the men came out of the boys' room, George looked Derek up and down with a nasty smile. Jordan's smile was apologetic; he carried a small stack of folded, wrinkled papers in his hands. The boy didn't immediately register what the papers were. Then he understood. His skin set ablaze.

The boy reacted on pure instinct; he turned on Ryan. His right hand, with the freshly sharpened claws, wrapped around Ryan's throat and slammed him, head first, against the door of the shoe closet. Out of the corner of his eye, the boy noticed the men backing up against the hallway wall, looking ill at ease. He grinned. He picked Ryan up by his neck, not an easy feat since Ryan was almost a head taller, and pinned him against the closet door. With his free hand, he continued pounding the particle board, until it split. The boy let Ryan go, reached into the busted closet, and pulled out Ryan's shoes. Ryan was sobbing on the floor.

"Get lost!" the boy hissed, and tossed Ryan's shoes at him.

That's when, following George's orders, Jordan tackled him, knocking him to the floor.

Chapter 20

Six months after he went away, Emma received a call from a blocked number. She was lucky; she was the only one home. The man was brief; he wouldn't give her his name. He did give her a message, though. "He loves you. He is ok. He's sorry he hasn't written. He can't."

Emma reached for a pen, knocking her coffee over in the process.

"I'll write him, then! What's the address?"

"Don't bother." The man's voice sounded weary. "He won't get letters from anyone who hasn't been approved. Look, I'm risking a lot, calling you. He said to ask you if you'll wait. He said the answer has to come from you."

"How?"

"I've thought it through. You can post an ad in the paper. The personal ads in the classifieds are free, as long as you keep it under twelve words, and they are anonymous. Will you post your response?"

***

Emma called the local paper the next day and posted the free message, exactly twelve words long. "Phoenix I love you. I'll wait. It's okay. Me and you always." She gave her home address and her home phone number for reference. Then she held her breath.

Chapter 21

The sunlight beams pierced the morning darkness, scalding his eyelids. The sun jarred him awake. The boy raised his elbow in an attempt to shield his eyes, slid farther into the corner and curled into a ball, clinging to the darkness, the silence of the seclusion room.

A noise stirred him, the sound of the viewing window opening.

"Derek?" The boy recognized Jordan's voice. It sounded labored. "Hey, kid, are you okay?"

The boy pretended not to hear. It was Jordan who had confiscated his unfinished letters, Emma's poems. He could still see Jordan's twisted face, as the orderly took him down last night.

The boy didn't move. He was a hare at the feet of a fox. *Be still, be very still, and perhaps the predator will not know you are there. Perhaps it will go away.*

"Listen, Derek, you lucked out. Ryan's going to be okay. A few stitches, that's all."

Kids were starting to wander in the yard; the sound of their feet scuffling on the gravel permeating the basement.

The boy didn't breathe. He didn't move. He was a statue carved of ice; he was dead. *Emma's poems. Her smell. Lost, all lost.* He sank his teeth into his lip and shut his eyes tighter.

"Derek, what's her number?'

I must've misheard. The boy blinked hard.

"What's her number, Derek?'

"What do you care?" The boy spun around and crouched on the floor. He looked ready to pounce.

"I read your letters, kid. I can get a message to her."

The boy felt a sliver of hope stir inside him. It swelled, threatening to eclipse every last bit of sense he had left. *What would it mean – to reach her, touch her? To bury his face in her neck?* Then the suspicion returned. *What sort of a dirty trick is this? Do they want to drag her into this mess, too? No!*

The boy forced himself to turn his back on the door, to shut out hope and longing.

"Derek, you jackass, do you understand what the two of you have? I've spent my whole life trying to find someone. And you two, you are like the starstruck lovers!" Jordan shuffled his feet, pulled a napkin out of his pocket, and blew his nose. "I'm trying to help you here! But I need her number."

Somehow, Jordan's words, his awkwardness disarmed the boy. Suspicion faded and gave way to elation, which formed somewhere at his core, and gradually spread out to his limbs. *Perhaps my magic worked, after all, in some twisted way manifesting itself in the form of this shuffling, awkward man that drives a sky-blue Volkswagen bug with the Star Trek emblem hanging from the rearview mirror.* What did he have to lose, anyway?

The boy paused, making up his mind. "Four one four. Sixteen. Twenty-five. Ask her to wait for me, okay?" The boy hesitated, reluctant to give form to his fears. "Hey, Jordan? The answer needs to come from her, only her, you hear me?"

***

For most of the day the boy paced the floor of his cage, imagining himself a tiger at a zoo. There were the bars. There was a metal watering dish. There were the occasional bored spectators.

He must've fallen back asleep, because again he found himself chasing her car on a dusty road, gulping for air, sensing the pursuit behind him. At a desolate corner at the edge of town, he caught up with the car and peered in through the dirty passenger window. From behind the wheel, Dave smiled at him reassuringly.

Then he woke up, and it took him a few moments to remember where he was. The dream left a stale aftertaste in his mouth.

He scanned the room and found a paper plate with two halves of a peanut butter and jelly sandwich by the door, along with a packet of grape juice. One of the orderlies must've brought down his lunch while he slept. That bothered him. He used to wake at the slightest whisper, the sound of leaves rustling outside his window. This time, he slept right through the screech of the opening door. *This place is starting to take its toll on me,* he thought.

He spent the remainder of the afternoon rolling the sticky bread chunks into little balls. He soaked these in the juice and used them to plug the blinding holes in the wood.

***

The light in the room became dispersed; it hung in the air like a smoke cloud. It was getting noticeably cooler. Finally, he heard the creaking of the wooden basement stairs; then the viewing window slid open.

He ran up to the door.

"I got hold of her," Jordan said quietly. "She'll post an ad."

"A what?" The boy leaned in, bewildered.

"A personal ad. In the classifieds. She'll post her reply."

Jordan's words slowly sank in.

"When?" The boy's eyes lit up.

"Soon." Jordan yanked the napkin back out of his pocket and wiped the sweat off his forehead. "Listen to me, Derek. You need to learn to play along, or you'll always be stuck down here. I am not saying you should change who you are, but just pretend, blend in just to get through. Emma's waiting for you out there; do you understand what I'm saying?"

The boy nodded. Then a thought crossed his mind. "Jordan, which paper?"

The steps above their heads started creaking again. Jordan froze, blinked rapidly, and slid the viewing window shut. The boy, too, held still, straining to hear through the steel door.

"Jordan?" Dave sounded drained, surprised, and annoyed all at once. "What the hell are you doing down here?" The boy could visualize Dave tiredly waving off Jordan's explanation. "Good thing I tracked you down. George wants a word with you."

Chapter 22

When Emma got home from school that day, she found her mother waiting for her by the door. Natalia was leaning against the wall, her arms crossed.

"I got an interesting phone call this afternoon, Emma."

The girl tensed, uncertain what to expect.

"Apparently, someone from this household had placed a personal ad in the newspaper." Natalia surveyed her daughter's face before continuing. "Since I'm still married to your dad, it clearly wasn't me. So, of course, I told them it must've been a mix-up and cancelled the posting."

"Why?" Emma uncoiled. "Why would you do that, mom?"

"Because Derek is ill, Emma! There must be a reason they locked him up."

"How can you say that? You don't know him!" Emma's eyes were two shiny lakes of hurt.

"He's ill, Emma! I've always said there's something wrong with that kid! Leave him alone!"

Her mother's tone made Emma sick. She felt the nausea rising from her groin and snaking up her intestines. It burst forth in a torrent of choked sobs.

Natalia persisted. "Me and your dad, we work so hard to give you a good life here, a new start! And what do you do? You find some street kid to fixate on!"

Emma cringed. She doubled over, clutched at her stomach with both hands, and shot past her mother into the bathroom, slamming and locking the door behind her.

Natalia's reflexes were just a fraction too slow; she ran into the door with her shoulder, winced at the sudden pain, and then began rhythmically banging on the door. "Emma, leave Derek alone, or I swear to god, I'll send you back to Rio to live with your dad!"

Emma fell to her knees in front of the toilet, raised up her head and stared blindly at the ceiling. Her mother's voice flooded in, merciless in its finality. *I'm sorry, Phoenix,* Emma prayed silently, licking the tears off her cracked lips. *I'm so sorry, there's nothing I can do. If she sends me off to Rio, you'll never find me.* She closed her eyes and attempted to conjure up his image. She saw nothing. She felt nothing. She wished for silence.

Chapter 23

By the time the boy got out of seclusion again, Jordan was gone from the Farmstead. "He had family matters that needed his attention," he was told. There went his chance to speak with Jordan, to find out which paper he should look in. The boy bit his lip, but forced himself to walk away without further questions. Now, he had to find a way to get his hands on as many publications as possible. His only option was to keep a low profile, play along, and wait for an opportunity.

That opportunity presented itself in the form of his new roommate, Jared.

Jared had just turned eighteen. When he was fourteen his mother died, forcing him to move in with his father, Jeff Railey, a successful software firm executive. During his sophomore year of high school, Jared decided to treat the entire tenth grade to a trip to Cancun with his father's company card. It didn't take long for the firm's accountant to notice the discrepancy in the expenses. Soon after, Jared was shipped off to the Farmstead.

There seemed to be some sort of an arrangement between Jared's father and Dave. Jeff Railey treated the Farmstead as if it were a boarding school. For Jared's sixteenth birthday, his father had bought him a shiny red Mazda. Jared drove it to town and back on weekdays; he held a job at a local pizzeria. Once in a while, when the staff would catch Jared smuggling beer into the barracks, his punishment was limited to a verbal reprimand.

***

"Don't sweat it, Derek" Jared told the boy on their third night together, when he'd cautiously brought up his request. "Newspapers ain't no contraband." Jared's face lit up with a huge grin as he leaned in close. "But first, you have to tell me what the hell you need them for."

"Emma." He spoke her name out loud for the first time since he'd arrived at the Farmstead. He felt as if an old, festering wound finally opened, and all the pressure and pain slowly drained away. He told Jared most of their story that night, including her promise to post her response. He was careful to leave out Jordan's name.

"Your baby-girl, hmm?" Jared sat back on his bunk, closed his eyes, and smiled dreamily. "Yeah, man, I'll help you out, but she better be hot!"

The younger boy grinned back and nodded.

"You got a picture?" There was live interest in Jared's eyes.

"No," the other boy said. "I don't have anything of her left, they confiscated everything long ago." It was only partially a lie. Jared didn't need to know about his one remaining treasure, the shirt Emma had made for him. He had buried it at the edge of the football field during his failed escape attempt.

Jared nodded and pulled out his wallet.

"Here is mine." He produced a faded, creased photo of a pretty Latino girl. "That's my Layla. Boobs like these," Jared traced the ample outline in the air, "and butt like this."

"Where's she now?"

"Cali."

"And you're here? Aren't you worried she'll forget you?"

"Nah. We've been together since before my mom died." Jared smiled and shook his head. "Layla's a good girl and anyhow, I call her whenever I'm in town."

***

Jared kept his word. He brought the boy newspapers by the sacksful. At night, they would look through the ads together by the light of Jared's tiny pocket flashlight. A few weeks into it, the boy talked Jared into calling Emma's house. The phone number had been disconnected. They didn't know what that meant. Meanwhile, Jared relayed to him all his latest conversations with Layla: Layla went shopping with her girlfriends; Layla dyed her hair; Layla bought a Chihuahua puppy and named him Pepper.

And still, there was nothing from Emma.

The boy started school again at the on-site Farmstead facility. The studying helped him pass the time. There were the weekly group-therapy sessions, "group-fucks," as Jared liked to call them. In the afternoons, the boy hung out with Jared in the activity room, or out on the field, hiding behind an old shed, smoking hand-rolled cigarettes. The other kids gave them their space.

One time, when the boy was out by the shed smoking by himself, he almost got plowed over by Dave himself. The therapist was marching across the field on some errand of his own without paying much attention to where he was going. For a few seconds, the two eyed each other. Then the boy panicked and opted to run. As soon as he saw Jared again, he pulled the older boy aside.

"I know he saw me, we were this close." He approximated the distance with his hands. "I think I'm really screwed, man."

"Nah." Jared shook his head. "I wouldn't worry 'bout Dave. He ain't that bad. He's just a lonely sad fuck trying to be cool."

There were more homecalls. His mother kept on promising to come up and visit as soon as his grandpa gave them the money to fix the van. She told him stories about Aunt Tonya's wedding, and Uncle Robert's knee surgery, and yet another house his grandfather had purchased. Her chatter wore the boy out; he tried to keep the conversations short.

"I hate talking to my folks," he'd complain to Jared afterwards. "What's there to talk about?"

Jared would shrug and shake his head. "What's there to talk about with my old man?"

Chapter 24

The summer had come and gone, and then another winter. Emma's pain diminished to a dull vortex of hurt. Her eyes stung, but there were no tears in them now. Only once in a while she would swallow, as if something was stuck in her throat. The world around her came through in shades of gray.

Emma kept asking herself what went wrong. *Why hasn't he come, why hasn't he found me, carried me away, as he promised? Has he forgotten me, forgotten his own magic, has he found someone else to feed his fire?* She was sure he had to be out by now.

She begged her mother to allow her to get some medical help for the depression that she was slowly sinking into, but it was no use. "Depression is a disease that you don't have," Natalia would tell her. "You're feeling down. It happens. Get ahold of yourself, stop dwelling on the past. Exercise more, get more fresh air."

Emma did neither. She took to smoking instead. Veiled in the blue smoke, she watched the magic and hope slowly drain from her universe.

She no longer jumped at the sound of a ringing phone. Her mother had changed the landline number shortly after the newspaper incident. "The solicitors were driving me crazy," Natalia told her daughter. Emma suspected that her mother's real purpose was to cut off any possible communication with him.

The last time Emma heard from him was six months ago, when she received a letter. "I think they're killing me in here," he wrote. "Where are you, Emma?" And that was all. The envelope had no return address.

What does he expect of me? Emma remembered thinking. *What can I do?*

Her mother's threat of sending her back to Rio de Janeiro had done its job. Her hands were tied.

***

A few weeks before Emma's graduation, Janna stopped her in the school hallway. "Come to my office," the counselor said. "I need to talk to you."

Emma obeyed. For the past two years Janna had been her lifeline, the only adult who hadn't lied to her and hadn't judged her.

When they got in, Janna shut and locked the office door.

"Sit down."

Emma sat down in the chair and watched as Janna dug through the top drawer of her desk. The counselor produced a folded piece of paper.

"I know I'm crossing the line here, but you are almost eighteen, Emma." Janna hesitated. "I promised you I'd check around. A friend of mine finally got back to me. I'm pretty sure this is where Derek is being held."

Emma swallowed, hard; it felt as if she was choking. *So, he is still locked up, after all,* she thought. *It's no use.*

"This … means a lot, Janna, it does. But I just can't. My mom will kill me." Emma hung her head. Then a thought crossed her mind, and she glanced back up at the counselor. "Could you?" The girl left the thought unspoken.

The woman shook her head. "No. It's out of the question. I'll lose my accreditation, my teaching license. Sweetheart, I've done all I can."

sat, facing each other, and listened to the students' s outside the office door.

erstand, Janna. I really do. Thank you." Emma got up. "I better get to class." She looked at , and saw sadness and pity in the counselor's . She turned for the door.

Emma." Janna stopped her. "Take this, just in case you change your mind." She handed the girl the paper.

"Yes," Emma mumbled and shoved the paper in her pocket. "Yes, of course." She walked out, in a daze. She wandered to a window, and stared out, out past the school fence and the encircling street, past the horizon. Her mind was spinning.

She finally knew where he was. *What difference does it make now*, she thought. *What am I supposed to do? Break into the place, guns blazing, break him out? And take him where? My mom's house?* This was nonsense.

It's been nearly two years. A lot has changed. She certainly wasn't the same naïve girl he had left behind. She doubted he was the same. She wondered if he even remembered her name.

No, she thought. *I can't do this to myself. I can't do this to my mom.* She took the paper out of her pocket and glanced at the address. *Another state, an unfamiliar town.*

She made up her mind. This was out of the questio

Slowly, deliberately, she tore up the paper to g the temptation.

Her eyes felt dry.

Chapter 25

He was worried about Jared, who hadn't been himself the past few days. Withdrawn and moody, he had even stopped bringing newspapers back from town. At night, Jared hardly slept. He'd lie awake and stare at the ceiling, flipping Layla's photo in his fingers.

The younger boy tried asking what was wrong.

"Not sure yet, man." Jared shrugged and slumped down on his bunk. "I'll tell you when I got it figured out."

On Thursday, Jared got back to the Farmstead in a particularly foul mood. "I need to see Dave," he said as soon as he walked in. "Derek, do you know if he's in his office?" Not bothering to wait for the boy's answer, Jared turned and marched off down the hall.

The younger boy waited several minutes, then followed. He crouched by the office door, and listened. The conversation must've been short, as he caught only the tail end.

et rid of

"It's just a week! I promise I'll be right back here." Jared raised his voice. "Pops, please, just once can't your damn business trip wait?"

There was a short pause, and then Jared's voice roared up again. "Fine, pops. Fuck you, then!"

The boy by the door quickly backed down the hallway.

He watched as Jared stormed out, watched Dave follow him. The two stopped. Jared's face was flushed red. Dave leaned forward and placed his hand on Jared's shoulder. For a few minutes, Dave spoke, then Jared broke the contact and walked away.

Dave was left standing in the empty hallway, his arm still half raised. He shook his head and looked around. He saw the boy, watching.

***

At dinnertime that night, they found themselves at the same table with Ryan.

Ryan's eyes were glistening; there was a hint of color in his cheeks. He was surrounded by a group of younger kids. They listened as he talked.

"The house is like three stories high, and mom's swimming pool is bigger than this room." Ryan pointed around. "And there's a gardener that lives on the property, and a maid to watch the house when she's on tour."

"Yep. And her boyfriend's Henry Ford," Jared interjected, an unkind spark dancing in his eyes.

"Wrong, Jared. Mom don't need no sugardaddy, like you do," Ryan retorted. It seemed that the prospect of an upcoming home-visit made him forget his most recent visit to the hospital. "She makes good money."

"Yeah, fucking guys like my dad," Jared murmured under his breath.

Some of Ryan's groupies couldn't keep back a giggle.

"Whatever, man!" Ryan was furiously blushing head to toe. He turned to his friends. "He don't know what he's talking about!"

"Ryan, baby," Jared's voice crept, like a lizard. "You've been here, what, nine years, last I checked? Newsflash. Your mother doesn't want you, sweetheart."

"She does!" Ryan stood up, his fists clenched and his chin quivering. "Ask Dave! She's coming up tomorrow!"

"Right." Jared yawned and turned away. "Just like she did last year, and the one before, and – you remember? – the one before that. Save it, Ryan."

"My mother. Is. Coming." Ryan was talking to Jared's back. He looked around blindly, then bit his lip and ran out of the room.

***

"Derek?" Jared whispered that night, after the orderlies had finished their evening rounds.

"Yeah?" The younger boy rolled over and propped himself up on one elbow.

"I can't get hold of Layla," Jared said in a hoarse whisper. "Five days now. I think she split."

"Don't think that. She could be busy."

"Nah. I've called and called and the phone goes straight to voicemail. Something's up, man. I can feel it."

They were both quiet for a bit, then Jared sat up on his bunk.

"I need to get back to Cali. I need to know what's going on there."

The other boy just listened.

"Dave even let me call home, out of turn," Jared spat onto the floor. "My pops said no way."

"So what are you thinking?"

"I can't just sit here. No way. Not while she...while she..." He made a strange noise, like a mouse caught in a trap. Still, he went on. "Come with me, Derek. We'll swing by, see your baby-girl."

The younger boy thought it over.

"I can't, Jared. Emma never posted anything, remember? I doubt she even wants me. And where would I go, her mom's house?"

"Maybe she did and we just missed it. We could find out." Jared was nearly pleading.

"I can't," the younger boy said, with a resolved sigh. "If I run now, I'll have to keep on running, or they'll catch me, and then I'm stuck for good."

"Cool." Jared nodded and lay back down.

Minutes ticked by.

"Derek?" Jared rolled back over to face the boy. "Write her a letter. I'll mail it."

"Her number's changed. She probably moved."

Jared shrugged. "So what? Maybe it'll get forwarded. You can't just give up on her, man. Write her."

Chapter 26

Three weeks after her high school graduation, Emma met Jack. She took up a part-time job at the campus bookstore that summer, as she waited for the fall semester to start. She was out back, smoking, when she was startled by the clanking of approaching boots.

Emma turned around and found herself face-to-face with a tall man. She slowly examined the stranger, starting at the tips of his cowboy boots, up to his wrangler jeans, his short-sleeved brown button-up, then back down to the tattoos on his arms. Something about the man struck a familiar chord. He had tattoos of wolves and tigers; of things clawed, winged, and fanged.

The man tipped his black cowboy hat to Emma. "Mind if I join you, miss?" His blue eyes sparkled at her.

Emma felt herself choking on memories and longing. She just stood there, and stared at the man, unable, unwilling to let go of the elusive iridescent blue.

The man's face lit up with a boyish smile. "I don't believe we've been properly introduced." He held out his hand. "I'm Jack."

Chapter 27

The boy sat on his bunk and toyed with the fluorescent mini flashlight that Jared had given him before skipping town. His eyes were focused on the blue dot that danced on the opposite wall, just above Jared's empty bed. It turned and swirled, vanished and reappeared. The boy could hear men's voices at the other end of the hall, but couldn't make out the words. He strained, hoping to catch scraps of the conversation.

There was nothing else to do. All the boys had been confined to their bedrooms since lunchtime, when Mark informed George that Ryan was also missing. The Farmstead went into lockdown mode; a sense of rising hysteria hung over the barracks. Outside the window, the sun was just beginning to set.

***

First, Jared hadn't shown up for the Friday evening lineup, leaving his roommate to deal with the aftermath. George had summoned the boy to his office and questioned him for hours. It was a waste of time. The boy lied stoically, insisting that he knew nothing about

Jared's whereabouts, had no idea why Jared would run away, or what could have upset him.

"Why don't you ask Dave instead?" the boy told George. "I saw them arguing last night."

In the end, George had no choice but to believe the boy and let him go.

On the way back to his room, the boy had wandered past Dave's office. The therapist's door was partially open, and he noticed that Ryan was still there, leaning back in his chair, his eyes closed. Ryan had been sitting there since that morning; he was waiting for his mother to show up. He was there again the following morning, as all the boys rushed past to get their breakfast, and after, when everyone went off to do their daily chores. By lunchtime, Ryan was gone.

Mark had come in during lunch and pulled George aside. The boy, with a grim satisfaction, recalled the panic that slowly spread over George's stubbly face. Mark kept his voice low. He must've asked a question; he leaned in close to George, raised his eyebrows. George waved him off.

"That's the least of our worries." George's voice carried through the room. "She's cancelled, as always."

Then came the announcement, followed by the uproar; the Farmstead seemed to echo its owner's moods. Disorder ensued. The staff ran about, ushering the kids to their bedrooms.

By evening, the general excitement gave way to boredom. There was nothing to do.

Minutes oozed by.

Alone in his room, the boy tried to guess how far Jared and Ryan could be by now. Jared had a car. Ryan had only his shoes, he was likely walking. The boy wondered if they would make it. He watched the bright blue dot dancing on the opposite wall. Outside, the sun had almost set. It was the middle of summer.

***

They brought Ryan back on Sunday. From his window, the boy saw an officer help Ryan out of the car, saw George sign the paperwork. The boy could see Ryan's face, red and flaky with sunburn. Ryan's jeans, up to his knees, were caked in mud; his prized sneakers – mere rags now. His shirt was torn at the collar; a rash ran up his left arm. He was covered in nicks and scratches. But it was Ryan's eyes that shocked the boy the most. They expressed no fear, no anguish, no spite. They expressed nothing.

***

Monday morning, Jared's car was towed back to the Farmstead. Its hood gaped wide, like the mouth of a dying fish. The headlights were gone, leaving behind the mangled wires of empty eye sockets. The cabin itself seemed crunched, bunched up like a miniskirt on a girl's butt. The car no longer had a windshield.

That Saturday, Jeff Railey came by the Farmstead to collect his son's belongings. He didn't say much to Derek, or anyone else, for that matter. His eyes were red and swollen.

***

By the following Monday, life on the Farmstead was mostly back to normal. The kids went about their daily chores. Classes resumed.

Late Monday afternoon, the boy walked into Dave's office and slammed the door shut. Dave looked up from his paperwork, startled.

"Derek, sit down." Dave gestured at a chair. "You must be pretty upset; I know you and Jared were close."

"So were you, from what he told me," the boy spat back.

Dave's eyebrows shot up. "Not like that!"

The boy dismissed him. "I know." He ignored Dave's invitation and kept on standing. "Yeah. I'm upset."

"About Jared?" the therapist nodded.

That was one major understatement. The boy smirked bitterly. He *was* upset; upset about Jared, upset about his so-called parents, and – he wasn't about to tell Dave about that – he was upset about that morning.

Right after breakfast, he'd snuck down into the basement. He tip-toed down the wooden stairs, slowly slid the viewing window open, and peered in.

Ryan was sitting on the floor, with his back to the door, and gently rocking his body back and forth.

"Ryan?" The boy was hoping for a response, any response, but there was none. Ryan kept on rocking; he didn't skip a beat.

The boy was certain Ryan had heard him just fine, so he went on anyway. "Ryan, it's me, Derek. Look, I just want to say I'm sorry. About before."

Outside the room, the wind raged; it battered and slammed against the glass. The glass shuddered. Derek could feel the vibrations within his body.

Inside, in the seclusion room, Ryan rocked back and forth, back and forth, back and forth.

Derek paused, struggling to put what he felt into words. "Ryan, I'm sorry about your mom. I…" He paused again, and thought about Jared. He thought about Emma. He forced himself to finish the phrase. "I know what it's like to wait for someone who isn't coming."

Inside the cage, the kid stopped rocking.

Derek held his breath. His heart was aching. The wind continued thrashing outside.

"Leave me alone, Derek," Ryan said. He resumed the rocking motion.

***

That was that morning. Now it was afternoon, and Derek stood face-to-face with Dave, both hands firmly planted on the therapist's desk.

"I didn't come here to talk about Jared. He wasn't the only one with someone on the outside, waiting."

"Okay." The therapist was inching away. "Why are you here?"

"I need to ask you a question."

"Okay." The therapist listened, while closely watching the boy's face.

"What do I need to do to get out of here?" Derek enunciated each word.

The therapist visibly relaxed. He smiled. "You are a smart kid, Derek, and you've been making great progress lately. I'm sure you have it figured out."

The boy swayed. He steadied himself. "I didn't come here to play games, Dave. So cut out the crap and spell it out for me."

"Okay." Dave shrugged. "You need to drastically improve your academic and athletic performances. You need to be diligent in your daily chores." He counted on his fingers as he spoke. "You need to show respect to your elders and your peers. Most importantly, you need to exhibit a sincere understanding of your past mistakes and a genuine desire to improve." He stopped.

Derek nodded and walked out of the room.

He returned in less than five minutes with a mud-encrusted grocery bag. "She gave me this a few days before I got thrown into this shit hole. It's all I have left of her." Derek placed the bag on the therapist's desk, right on top of his papers and reviews, and proceeded to shake the dirt off his hands onto Dave's carpeted floor.

Dave cautiously inspected the bag, then dumped its contents out on the desk. Inside the bag was a rotten wet T-shirt, which still maintained some of its blackish-grayish color. Although the fabric was heavily stained and soiled, the orange flecks of paint still clung to the cotton fibers, outlining an image of a bird on fire.

"Sincere enough for you?" Derek asked grimly. He turned to the door.

"Derek!" Dave called out after him.

The boy turned back around and watched as the therapist dug through his briefcase.

The man took out a cigarette pack, pulled out three cigarettes, and held them out to the boy. "Go ahead, take these," he said. "You've had a shitty couple of weeks."

Chapter 28

Emma clung to the armrests of her window seat as the airplane rocked back and forth, back and forth, back and forth. Next to her, Jack snored away peacefully, his tall frame contorted, conforming to the limitations of the economy class. It was late autumn; they were on their way to Colorado to meet Jack's mother.

Emma had been on rough flights before, but nothing like this. The plane rolled from one wing to the other. It shuddered. The paneling flexed; Emma could feel the vibration in her body. Nausea was rising up in her throat. She clenched her teeth.

The plane took a dip.

A few rows back, an infant let out a shrill cry.

Every time the plane changed altitudes, Emma's ears popped. *It's just bad weather,* she tried to calm herself, *it's going to pass.* Her hands were growing numb from grasping the armrests.

The plane dove down sharply, then straightened again.

Emma held her breath, held back the squeal that almost escaped her lips. Her fear was childlike; she needed somebody strong and sure to comfort her. Instinctively, she reached for Jack's hand.

He shifted and mumbled, then took his hand away.

She bit her lip.

Thrashed by the wind, the airplane swayed left and right. The child in the back kept crying out in sync with the plane's motion. Luggage rattled inside the airplane's belly.

"Baby!" Emma gripped Jack's arm and shook him, trying to wake him up.

He coughed. The snoring stopped.

"Jack!"

"Huh? What?" He partially opened one eye.

"Please wake up, I am scared!"

He blinked at her, not comprehending what she meant.

At that moment, the airplane, hit by another wave of frozen air, dropped a few feet.

Emma gasped. She stared at Jack, pleading with her eyes.

At last, he figured out what was wanted from him. "Don't you be scared, babe, it's just a rough spot. We'll be fine." He adjusted his pillow, glanced down at Emma, and noticed that her expression hadn't changed. "I'm tired babe," he mumbled and patted her on the arm. "Try to get some sleep." A few moments later, Jack was snoring again, leaving Emma on her own.

The plane continued its dance between the clouds: up, down, left, right, up again.

It's only a disturbance, Emma attempted to reason with herself, but that did little to ease her fear. Her ears were ringing; she felt motion sickness creeping in. The airplane dipped and shuddered. Someone's briefcase slid across the compartment above her head.

Emma braced her head against the headrest and closed her eyes.

She visualized the phone ringing at her mother's house, her mom picking it up, gasping at the news, and slowly sliding to the floor along the kitchen wall, ashen-faced, her hand still clutching the receiver. Then Emma thought of Jack's yet unknown mother, a merry, pleasant-sounding woman, humming away happily as she went about her cooking and tidying up her home, awaiting her son's arrival.

And what about me? she thought. *My plans, my future, the classes I'm supposed to take next semester?* Her terror was irrational, but it felt real. *I am not ready,* Emma shouted silently. *I don't want to die!* Her cheeks were wet. Feeling the panic build inside her, Emma reached out to the one being she had always trusted, invoking an old, half-forgotten ritual.

She prayed to Phoenix.

My love, she pled. *My love, wherever you are now, please hear me. It's been too long, I know, but I really, really need you right now. In the name of everything we once shared, and everything that was taken from us, please, don't let me wreck, carry me through on your dark wings! There's so much left undone. I'm so scared.*

She chanted the words again and again, like a mantra, as she slowly sank into a gentle, welcoming darkness.

***

Two hours later, when the plane safely touched down in Colorado, Emma smiled. "Thank you, Phoenix," she whispered into the retreating darkness.

In the seat next to her, Jack was just starting to wake up.

Chapter 29

Another homecall.

Derek sat in Dave's office and stared blankly at the white apparatus before him. He was rehearsing the conversation in his head. The phone rang, and as always, the loud sound caught him by surprise.

He picked up the receiver.

"Derek!" His mother was fretting again. "It's so wonderful to hear your voice, honey!"

"It's nice to hear from you as well," Derek said flatly.

His stepdad joined in. "Hey, buddy! How'd you like your present?"

Derek looked down and lovingly patted the sleeve of his new brown bomber jacket. "That's very nice of you. Thank you."

"It's what you wanted, right? We were worried that we got it wrong. You always used to like those black leather coats, remember?"

"It's fine, mom."

"Oh, good! We really wanted to do something very special for your eighteenth birthday, honey." His mother rambled on. "Your grandpa took us out shopping for you this year, did you know?"

"We wanted to show you just how proud we all are of you," his stepdad interjected.

"Honey, we have great news," his mother, again. "Grandpa borrowed us some money to fix the van. We want to come up and see you next weekend!"

"That would be nice," Derek said, keeping his voice even and upbeat.

"How's school? We've heard you're doing fantastic!"

"School's good. Dave said I can probably graduate with honors."

"Buddy! Those are wonderful news!"

"And are you still making friends? How's that boy you've mentioned? Jared, I think?"

"Jared's doing great, mom." Derek clenched his teeth, holding back a growl. "Just great."

"Oh, that's nice. He sounded like such a nice boy."

"Yes, yes. Look, mom," Derek cut into her wordflow. "Class is starting soon. I really gotta go now." He hung up the receiver and remained sitting, lost in thought.

The door opened and Dave walked in. "How'd that go, kiddo?" Dave rested his hand on Derek's shoulder.

"As usual." Derek shrugged and glanced up at the therapist. "Long and pointless."

"But you did well! Remember, all you have to do is give people what they need. It's simple, isn't it?"

"Yeah, until they randomly decide to show up at your doorstep for the first time in two years."

"What do you mean?" Dave's eyes narrowed.

"They want to come up next weekend, Dave." Derek sighed heavily. "Do I really have to see them?"

Dave relaxed and flashed the boy an encouraging smile. "Well, I for one am not about to force you."

Derek grinned back.

"I have an idea." Dave paused for a minute, and then winked. "Say, Derek, how'd you feel about snowboarding? Ever been to Lake Tahoe?"

A huge smile lit up Derek's face.

Chapter 30

Emma was in her second lab of the day, when she felt her phone go off. She glanced at it and didn't recognize the number. But then, for all she knew, it was Jack calling her from some gas station, his truck broken down again, his phone – dead.

She snuck out into the hallway and dialed the number back.

"Emma? It's me." The voice was milk and vodka.

"Phoenix?" She had to steady herself. "Phoenix! How'd you get my number?"

"I tracked Brandon down. Remember him? Emma, listen. I'm at the airport, terminal two. I need to see you."

I really should think this over, Emma thought, as she started up her car. *Is seeing him, now, a good idea?* she thought, as she sped down the freeway.

Her phone rang. She glanced at it.

It was Jack.

She hit the 'ignore' button, and felt around the passenger seat for her purse. It wasn't there. *Shit! I must've left it at the lab.*

Her phone rang again.

Jack.

She let it go to voicemail, as she sped up to pass a slow moving car.

Her phone rang. Jack. She groaned and hit 'end call.' She was almost to the airport exit.

Ring. Jack. Ring. Jack. Ring. Jack.

"Fuck!" Emma said.

She rolled down the window and tossed the phone out.

***

Emma parked the car on the second level of the parking lot and ran to terminal two, scanning for him out front of the building. It was midday. There was a small crowd of travelers by the entrance. It took her a while to spot him; he looked so different now, with his hair cut short and sun-bleached, his face glowing with a healthy tan. He was wearing a pair of blue jeans and a brown leather jacket. He was alone near the curb, smoking, and Emma strained to glimpse his eyes. When she finally did, she noticed that they were pale-blue.

Then he saw her and at last his eyes flared up with the familiar sapphire. "Emma!"

"Phoenix!" She ran up to him and threw her arms around his neck.

He picked her up and spun her around, laughing.

"How'd you manage to get out?" she asked eagerly, as soon he sat her back down on the ground. She watched his eyes slowly fade back to pale-blue.

"I'm not out yet, just passing through on a field trip."

"Then how?" She shaped her fingers into a semblance of a phone and held them to her ear.

He smiled down at her. "My therapist's cool. He told me I should call you." He put his cigarette out and reached in his pack for another.

Just passing through? Should call me? Her head was spinning. "I need a cigarette." Emma held out her hand.

"You smoke now?" He glanced at her sideways, his eyes narrowing.

"Yep." Emma shrugged.

"You shouldn't. I'm trying to quit." He handed her a clove anyway.

She lit up and at once choked on the potent tobacco, her eyes watering from the bittersweet smoke and memories that rose up like bile in her throat.

"Are you okay?" He reached over and took her by the hand. Gently, he lifted her fingers up to his lips.

She fought to calm her breathing. *They may have taught him to act like them, but they couldn't make him forget me.* She held on to his hand, afraid he wasn't real.

For a while they were both silent, content with just the touch, just the proximity.

Then the absurdity of the situation dawned on her. "Phoenix, what are we doing here?" She looked into his eyes. "You're eighteen; they can't legally hold you anymore! Let's go! My car's across the street! I've got my own place now." In her excitement, she forgot Jack entirely.

Next to them, a short pudgy man in a brown leather jacket got up and put out his cigarette. "We should get going, Derek, or we'll miss our plane," he said in their direction. "You still want to go to Tahoe, right?"

"One second, Dave," Derek said.

The man nodded at him, then Emma, and headed inside the terminal.

"Phoenix?" Emma blinked.

Derek smiled at her reassuringly. He brushed her hair away from her face, leaned in, and kissed her on the forehead. "I've been really looking forward to this trip, love. I've got to go." He gently let go of her hand, and said, "I'll call you." Then he turned and followed the man inside.

She stood, alone, on the sidewalk and stared at the sliding door.

Epilogue

Emma was walking to her car from the corporate headquarters, running through her to-do list in her head. *Call about the electric bill. Oh, and call mom when I get back to my place. But first, stop and get some dog food.* Exhausted after the three-hour board meeting, she was eager to see Red's wagging tail. It was midsummer. The air felt hot and stale. Her purse strap was starting to cut into her shoulder; the briefcase she carried was slipping from her grip. Emma stopped in the center of the sidewalk, to readjust.

When she looked up again, she saw him.

He stood near a coffeeshop entrance. His back was turned to her, but she still recognized the slope of his shoulders, his posture. Cautiously, almost inaudibly, she called out "Phoenix!"

He spun around. His eyes met hers and lit up with recognition. "Emma?"

And that was all it took. She dropped both the briefcase and the purse on the asphalt and ran to him, holding out her hands, afraid he would again slip through her fingers.

He wrapped her in his arms and pulled her close. For an eternity, they stood in the middle of the sidewalk among the sea of people that flowed all around them, her cheek against his cheek, each heartbeat echoing the other.

"It's you! It's you..." she whispered over and over into his ear. "My god! How long have you been out?"

For a split second longer, he still held her close. Then, slowly, he disentangled himself from her and held her out at arm's length. "Quite a while," he said evenly.

"Derek?" A tall blonde woman had emerged from inside the shop, and was now staring at them with heavily lined eyes. "Derek, who is this?" she demanded.

He backed away from Emma, towards the other woman, his eyes expressionless. "No one, honey. This lady was just asking for directions."

"I saw you hugging her!" Hurt and indignation twisted the blonde's face.

"You were mistaken, honey." He placed his hand on the woman's shoulder reassuringly. "And you're tired. We should go home." He turned and started to walk away. A few steps later he stopped and glanced back at Emma, his eyes scalding her with a cold blue flame. His face distorted. "You know, Emma, Dave *was* right. You never bothered waiting for me!" He flung the words at her, then turned again, and kept on walking. The blonde shot Emma a frightened look and hurried after him.

Emma watched him walk away, her eyes blurry with tears. She was shaking. She couldn't think of anything to say.

***

Instead of going home, Emma drove to his parents' house. She didn't know why, but it seemed that they, again, were her only thread.

Lida answered the door for her, looking thinner, frailer; her hair was starting to turn gray.

"Gary!" Lida shouted back into the house. "Gary, come look who's here!" She ushered Emma inside, brushed the newspapers off the old couch.

"You've seen Derek?" Lida asked the moment all three of them sat down. "How's he doing?"

"He seemed okay." Emma tried to comfort Lida with a smile. "How've you been?"

Lida didn't say anything. She was staring off into space, lost in her thoughts.

Gary sat up and wrapped his arm around his wife, protectively. "We aren't doing too bad. Thanks for asking." He started coughing.

Lida seemed still lost in a world of her own. "Do you know, Emma, he hardly talks to us, since he got out? We haven't heard from him since last Christmas." The woman's lips were trembling. She paused and held her hands up to her chest. "I keep on thinking, was there something we could've done different?" She turned and looked at Emma. "What could we do?"

Emma gently took the older woman by the hand and looked her in the eyes.

"Please, Lida, don't blame yourself. Even I don't blame you for doing what you did. He was a difficult kid. You had to send him off."

"He was a handful, my boy, wasn't he, Gary?" Lida smiled at some old memory. "But I would've never sent him away." She squeezed Emma's hands.

Emma stared at Lida, bewildered. "I don't understand."

Lida hesitated.

Gary gently patted his wife's back. He coughed again.

Lida tried to explain. "You remember how he liked to wear those funny clothes to school and that silly face paint of his?"

Emma nodded.

"Derek and Brandon – you do remember little Brandon, don't you Emma? – they thought it'd be cute to dress that way for church one day. They always were up to something, those two troublemakers." Lida shook her head. "My dad, Derek's grandpa, he was so embarrassed! Do you remember, Gary?"

"Well, yeah." Gary sighed. "Then they snuck out during the service. Lida's dad found them smoking out back. He told me he saw them holding hands."

Lida nodded. "Dad told me Derek needed help. He said he'd see to it." Her voice broke. She brought her right hand up to her heart. "I was beside myself!"

"Hold on a minute." Emma stopped them. "That makes no sense, Lida. You are his mother. If you were against sending him there, why didn't you just go get him?"

"It's okay, honey." Gary nodded. "You can go ahead and tell her now."

"You see, Emma," Lida struggled. She was searching for the right words. "I was a wild child when I was young. Love and peace and whatnot. And I was very young when I had Derek." She blushed. "My dad, he was furious when he found out." Lida tensed up, and reached for Gary's hand.

"What Lida's trying to say," Gary stepped in, "is that we never have had custody of Derek. His grandpa did."

Emma stared and stared. It wasn't sinking in. Then she jumped up. "Does Derek know this?"

"No!" Lida grabbed the young woman's hands. "No, no. I've never told him. God forbid. I don't want him to hate me!"

"Why didn't you fight for custody, when you got older?"

Lida didn't say a word. She was shaking.

"Sweetie, why don't we take a break while I go fetch your medicine?" Gary's voice was raw and tender. He turned to Emma. "Emma, you wouldn't mind getting Lida some water, would you?"

Emma silently followed him into the kitchen, her mind racing. Gary handed her an empty coffee mug and pointed at the tap. "Tap water is just fine," he said loudly, then leaned in close to Emma and whispered, "She tried, so her dad had her committed and declared unfit. Emma, please, she isn't well. Her heart…"

"Did someone call my name?" Lida called out from the living room.

Before she left, Emma asked to see his old room. It seemed much larger now, with the bed gone. In its place, Gary's brand new computer desk sat up against the wall. Beige curtains swayed against the modest window. There were no murals on the walls; they'd been painted over white. No monsters breathed in the corners now. The room was brightly lit, pristine, and dead.

Emma said her goodbyes and headed out to her car. She was reaching for the door handle, when Lida came running out after her.

"Emma! I almost forgot." Lida hurried along the driveway. "Here! We never got the chance to give this to him." She handed the young woman a small, neatly wrapped parcel. "I thought that you should have it."

Emma stared down at the package, unsure of what it was. She read the label:

To: Derek Upwall

Care of Mr. David Summerfield

The Boys' Farmstead

Across it, in a thick purple marker, someone had written: "Rejected. Return to sender."

Emma placed the package on the hood of her car and slowly peeled off the tape. One by one, she took out the contents, running her fingers over each item as she set it to the side. The pack of the clove gum. Emma smiled bitterly and bit her lip. The card. A wolf stared up into the sky at the majestic eagle overhead, still waiting.

Finally, Emma unwrapped the pendant and clasped the tiny silver phoenix in her hand. She looked up, as if searching for something. The heavens were serene. No dark wings disturbed the bright blue sky above her.

Emma started the car. Lida stood in the driveway, waving.

"Emma," she shouted, "If you see Derek again, please tell him that we miss him very much!"

"I will!" Emma shouted back with a reassuring smile.

As she turned the corner, she glanced down at the ornament clutched in her hand. *Forgive me, Lida.* Emma choked on the wave of tenderness she suddenly felt for the older woman. *Forgive me, but I will not see Phoenix again.* She forced her tears down, clenched the steering wheel, and headed home where Red was eagerly awaiting his afternoon walk…

Letters to Phoenix

"They were twins, and the hip crowd loved the perversity of that. Their mirror-image pornography was art."

Lost Souls, Poppy Z. Brite

First Letter

Phoenix,

Why are your wrists covered with scars, love? Is it hopeless for you? Does the night sky call? Do your wings ache? Can you fly?

***

Outstretched fingers touch

On the horizon of fear

Where you live.

***

Are you lost, too? Are you scared? Do I seem beautiful to you? When I smile, do you see my soul? Is your skin as fragile, as delicate, under the sun? Do you, too, dream of fear and sweat? Do you cry alone in your room, when no one can hear you?

Is the blood sweet?

***

Bluest network.

Lullaby cradling

Orgies

Of

Dead lovers.

IS IT SWEET?

***

Why are your wrists covered with scars, love? Why are your wrists covered with scars? Why scars?

***

I am as you are. I am you.

In anger and fear I am you.

This pain we share is what we are.

The lust and fear.

We are the outcasts.

We are the monsters.

We are hated.

Feared.

Copulating fervently

In the sky.

***

I am God. I created you. You are what I need.

You are a dream. My dream. My life. My emptiness.

Personified.

Second Letter

"Please, don't let me go," you said.

I had an appointment. I always keep my appointments.

We got in the car; the stereo wailed like a woman in childbirth. The wind clung to your hair with a violent hunger. We took off, me and you, in the car. We didn't talk during the ride – the stereo kept us apart with the gentle hands of a war surgeon, but your anger was tangible – a little insect, an earthworm. In the half light of the freeway, you looked like an iron statue, rigid and dark. I smiled because you were there. You were you.

I know your hair like I know any man's body. It is soft and dry and full of promises. That night, when I parked, you brushed it from your eyes in a brisk impatient gesture and once again said: "Stay."

I left. Because I wanted to, because I had to. Your blue-green mad eyes took a snapshot of me as you waved goodbye...

***

eyes blue-green

water green

blood blue

thick veins

blue eyes

paper skin

peel the flakes

cry for me

blue-green eyes

tears fly

paper doll

dry corn

blue-green

thoughtless eyes

just like mine

smile in lust

slam the wall

break the door

lose the key

shower wall

porcelain cold

paper thin

peeling skin

in your eyes

blue-green sky

i am gone

please don't cry.

***

Julie Deshtor

In your anger, the despair of a lonely pup shyly came to life. I watched you walk into the page – round back, marble shoulders, and a dark tangle of hair. When you disappeared, I started the car again and headed for the other house, into the other man's arms.

I cried all the way there, because the magic we shared died.

***

Children cry.

Children worship.

Children mate and birth children.

We have no mothers, no fathers, no lovers, no friends.

We are eternally free.

Sky free.

We wear masks because we ache.

Eyeliner outlines the pain.

Pain that defines us.

Pain that is sacred.

Touch my hand.

Dance with me.

Third Letter

Phoenix,

I am here, you are here, dance the night away, the pain calls and there are no consequences...

***

Black on black is the color: black walls, black clothes, black smoke. Painted skulls grin with orange teeth. Ghosts whisper softly in the corners. Music taunts their secrets with the drumbeat of the bass. Tender naked cables hug the stage with pale arms. Children sway. Mirror images wave their arms up and down in mock surrender.

***

From pain

lovers laugh.

Kiss wet faces.

Smeared makeup

from your face

on my lips.

***

Where we live there is only the
fear of our happiness.

For tomorrow is tomorrow
is tomorrow…

***

The day when we
lived died last night.

Are you leaving?

Will you take me with you?

Fourth Letter

Phoenix,

I pray to the Christian God and to the Father of Lies, to shield you, and to spare you from the light that surrounds you.

I pray to Luna, the Pale Mother, to guide you through the endless nights of loneliness.

May your hair always be dark and plentiful, and may your hands never wither, and may the sun always shine for you in the afternoons.

I pray, also, to the forces of darkness, those who fathered you, to strengthen you, and to deliver you from the terrible goodness of God.

I bid the owls and mosquitoes to carry my love to you, so you may return unharmed to our sweet neverland.....

***

When he walked out, he said: "I'll see you tomorrow."
His tomorrow never came. He left without her, spoiled
the future they had planned for so long.

All alone again.

The memories of all the people she had buried crowded
like ants in her head. Faces, smiles, bits of voices and
words.

Dead, all dead.

What was she supposed to do with those memories?

***

Beyond the return

> *only I will wait forever*

>> *for your anger.*

Fifth Letter

> "Who was born and
> murdered and resurrected
> inside that skull?"
>
> **Lost Souls**, Poppy Z. Brite

Phoenix,

*Is your favorite incense as sweet as mine, or is it bitter?
Do you burn your fingers lighting the matches? Does
the pain feel like a blessing? Does it hurt to burn in the
flame?*

*What is it like to live forever, love? Do you still believe
in God? Do you pray to Him? Or do you pray to fire?
What does it feel like to be trapped in this body? Do
your phantom wings ache? Do they burn?*

*Do you miss your lover? The universe? What does this
planet look like from eternity? Can you die? Are you
leaving?*

Will you take me with you?

(Will you take me with you?

    Will you take me with you?

        Will you take me with you?

            Will you take me with you?

                Will you take me with you?

                    Will you take me with you?

                        Will you take me with you?

                            Will you take me with you?)

***

Phoenix, Phoenix, Phoenix, the proud flame-bird! Will they make you human again?

Such a murderous crime, this…

P.S.

Phoenix,

I miss the sky we have created over the years of our loneliness. Sometimes I look up and I still see you there, wings spread, a broken child.
Beautiful.

***

I want to thank you for the years
you've waited outside of time,
for all the nights I knew that you were mine,
for the delusions we shared,
for your hands on my hips, your lips
still sugarcoated in my dreams I see your wings.
Your shadow follows me yet,
I close my eyes and I forget that you are gone.

***

"Touch my hand. Dance with me..."

Of Beasts and Men

In the middle of the night she woke from a nightmare and at once reached for him, placing her palm on his warm hip. She had dreamt that she was walking through the zoo with her mother.

They had already passed the monkey pavilion with its two noisy, curious gibbons, passed the flamingo pond, and had come across the tiger enclosure. The big cats were lazily sprawled about on the grass, warming their backs in the dull September sun. A large male yawned slowly, baring his teeth, and exposed the dark pink tunnel of the throat to the crowd. She pressed her face against the glass, trying to get a better look at the ivory white fangs, and that is when she noticed him.

He was sitting, cross-legged, on a large rock in the middle of the tiger enclosure, motionless, silent. The cats circled in a slow orange choreography, paying no attention to the human in their midst. When their eyes would occasionally fall on his body, they would stare through him with feline familiarity.

His head hung forward, his hair cascading over his face, yet she could tell that he was watching her, his blue-green eyes tracking her every movement. In the dream, silent like an old film, she remembered slamming against the glass, her lips moving without sound. Her mother's firm grip was dragging her, dragging her, dragging her away from the cage. A swarm of preschoolers suddenly manifested around her, picked her up like a wave, and carried her off. The cage that held him and the tigers grew smaller and smaller until it vanished from her view. Still, she kept yelling breathlessly.

***

She sat up, got up off the mattress, lightly, so as to not disturb his sleep, and tucked in the blanket to protect him from the chilly night air. For more than a month now they had been sharing the same bed every night, and yet the recurrent nightmare would not leave her alone. In the bathroom, she splashed cold water onto her face to chase away the dream, and brushed her hair. The house was silent, their roommates either asleep or gone for the night. She shut the bathroom door and shyly, like a newlywed, straightened her lavender nightgown, before heading back into the living room where they slept.

She was greeted by the barrel of his 9 mm.

He was lying on his back, his head propped up on a pillow. His blue eyes, though open, seemed strangely void. He aimed at her forehead, between her eyes. The gun was glowing a dim orange, reflecting the nightlight in the corner.

She stopped, mid-smile, and watched his chest rise and fall.

So this is how it begins, she thought absently.

His arm, bent at the elbow, seemed marble in the darkness. Not a single muscle twitched. If it weren't for his breathing, he would have appeared to be a perfect statue of a gunman.

She glanced about the room. The blanket she had tucked in so carefully only a few minutes ago had slipped off the mattress and fallen in a crumbled mess to the right side of him, on top of her discarded clothes. His leather jacket, one of the few possessions he had managed to acquire since his escape, hung over a chair. The curtains on the window were slightly open, allowing a satin stream of light from a street lamp into the room. The light contoured his face, traced his forehead and high cheekbones, reflected off his pupils. The peephole in the front door next to their makeshift bed glittered, like a tiny star, and she noticed that she had left the deadbolt unlocked.

She took a step towards the bed. The gun moved with her, maintaining a straight line; the shortest distance between the muzzle and her brain. She closed her eyes and waited. Nothing happened. She stood still, matching his breathing in an attempt to calm her own. As she watched his eyelashes flutter, watched him inhale and exhale at his slow, steady pace, she started to wonder if he was still asleep. She wanted to call out, "Derek, it's me!"

Instead, she began retreating before the hollow void of the barrel.

She moved slowly, so as not to startle him, inching her left foot off the floor, lowering it back down, toes first. She was careful not to slap the back of her slipper against the tile.

She repeated the same motions with her right foot, then the left again. She paused between steps to regain her balance. *Two. Three. Four. Five.* On the fifth step, she knocked over an empty beer bottle that someone had left on the floor. She almost fell. She caught herself. The bottle tipped and rolled across the tile, clanking loudly. The resonance echoed through the room.

He stirred.

She froze; her right hand on the floor, her left ankle twisted in its slipper. Her eyes dashed towards him like startled ferrets.

Slowly, he sat up, the gun still pointing in her general direction.

"Emma?" His voice was groggy. "Is that you?" He lowered the barrel. "Where are you, love?" Searching for her in the dark, he held out his other hand.

She sprang up and ran to him, grabbing onto his offered hand. Breathlessly, she collapsed into the bed.

As he rolled over towards her, he absentmindedly shoved the gun back underneath the pillow. He noticed that she was shaking.

"Come here, love, you're cold," he said dreamily and wrapped her in his powerful, lean body.

About the Author

Julie Deshtor grew up in the Soviet Union during the turbulent 90s, and moved to the United States shortly after the Soviet Empire collapsed in 1991. A bilingual author, Julie writes both fiction and poetry, as well as translating poetry and lyrics. She brings her rich cultural and life experiences to her fiction, exploring the psychological struggles of her characters with compassion and insight, as they navigate the murky waters of modern society.

Julie currently resides in Utah, USA. Her interests include art, world literature, zoology, anthropology, and urban subculture.